For all those who can't stop running. For all those who find themselves in the stories.

Ivy K.

Easter was her favorite holiday

short stories & poetry

She made me feel like I was standing in front
of a labyrinth but in complete darkness
And I even though I felt so lost, I also felt so
foolishly hopeful.
Maybe I could make it, maybe I can get
through this, I thought.

When I should have known

In my mother's kitchen, the television was on. The news anchor was talking about an elderly couple who had finally decided to get married in their late eighties. The screen switched to a video of two women in wheelchairs, and I noticed tears welling up in my eyes. I quickly wiped them away, not wanting to admit that I was crying. Why did it touch me so? Of course, the two of them were absolutely sweet, and the legalization of same-sex marriage was a historic event, but why did it bring me to tears? I had never cared much for marriage.

Maxima

The bell rings. Nico and Charlie have already packed their things. I'm, as always, much too slow. My mother often says that I'm a dreamer, and I wonder how something that sounds so beautiful could be meant negatively. "Jonathan, come on, we need to catch the bus," Nico nudges my upper arm lightly. I rub it. "I have my bike here; you can go without me." That was a (necessary) lie. I actually have to catch the bus, but I'm waiting for Maxima to come to my table.

I used to pray that she would talk to me, that she wouldn't fall in love with anyone else, and now, now I'm almost drowning in fear. I never know for sure if she's ashamed of me. She writes me notes, hides them under my desk, but never signs them with her name. That's why I still doubt that they really come from her. Sometimes I wonder if she could be ashamed of me. Then I remember that no one sees us together, and even if they do see us together, they don't notice us. But somehow, that's the good part of it, when no one cares about you. We don't have to hide anything, no one would believes us anyway, especially not me. No one talks about us, no one speculates. I'm invisible next to her. No one would ever think that she secretly likes me this way. No one sees us for what we are or could be. No one is jealous, no one is envious. And if they are, it's only our friendship that's considered too sudden.

She's actually coming over to me. I feel like I've been glued to the floor right there, i feel as if I glued myself there. When we talk, I often mix up syllables or entire words, nothing embarrasses me more.

How is tonight going to go? Is it even a kind of date, or does she just want to be friends with me? Does she expect me to kiss her? What an unimaginable process. What happens in the moments before a kiss? I've never been able to imagine that. And why the heck does it seem so easy for everyone else? I'm almost angry at her, but in reality, I'm just angry with myself. "I'm looking forward to later," she says, partly too softly but also somehow too loudly. I'm ready to take any kind of rejection instantly and mercilessly on myself. In my head, she cancels on me at exactly that moment. "See you later," she whispers and leaves.

Everything seems so fragile to me, I'm as uncertain as a cat that rubs against a stranger's legs. The bus is gone by now, but it doesn't bother me. I walk because today the silence is beautiful. I want to hum her name, say it, sing it. All day, over and over. I can think of her, I can dream of her whenever and wherever I want. Without even knowing, she's made everything better, every song, every color, every place.

And then, there was actually a kiss, don't ask me how, I can't reconstruct it myself, as if I wasn't there. "Somehow, I wish that had been my first kiss." "Why?" Why am I asking something like that, you fool. "I've kissed boys before you, but it never really felt right. It's somehow different with you. I have to admit that I was pretty nervous," she says, and I notice that I'm hovering a few inches above the ground.

All the time, the years I spent comparing every connection to ours, were, in retrospect, despite the defeats, the most beautiful of my life. I neither fought nor gave up; I waited. I waited, and in my imagination, she was waiting too, though unaware of it. Perhaps, at some point, she would meet me where I was already waiting with packed bags. In that interim, one can only endure it when one is sure of why.

The moment I knew I felt nothing but relieve, the fear came with the overthinking, but the moment I fell in love with her was pure.

The whole city was enchanted. It was a bit like how you see New York in a cheesy Christmas movie, compared to the real New York. Only I could perceive this magical version of the city. Everything was perfectly illuminated, and suddenly, I noticed all this beautiful details. Everything was shining so brightly, and I couldn't get enough of it. At some point, I realized that it wasn't the city that had been enchanted, it was me. Only me, unfortunately only me.

When the Lavender blossoms

Fatua had arranged herself with the fact that she could never speak the truth. Fatua was one of the fairies who were only believed when they lied. If she wanted something, if she wanted to achieve something, she had to weave a clever plan. If she let her guard down for a moment, the truth slipped out, and no one believed her. Fatua had been called a liar several times, and it seemed like no one in the entire fairy family, no one in the whole forest, was afflicted by the same curse. She made such an effort not to stand out, not to hurt anyone with her nature, but she didn't really want to keep betraying herself. And even though Fatua was extremely cautious and thought through every word, every gesture, the reputation of being a liar still stuck to her. Her wings and her dress were purple, which set her apart from everyone else. The other fairies had either blue or pink wings. The fairies' clothes and skirts always matched the colors of their wings. But Fatua's skirt was lavender, just like the blossom from which she hatched. No one else in her forest looked like her. No one believed her that fairies could hatch from lavender blossoms, she felt betrayed within her own circles. Furthermore, the legend held that fairies with this kind of attire were liars, that they never spoke the truth, and one should be cautious around them. Those who hadn't heard of this only thought that she wanted to stand out, that she didn't want to be like the others. Many of the other fairies ignored her, so she often felt invisible. She unintentionally stood out, yet it seemed she was never seen. What she revealed about herself was like a scar, a scar that reopened with every glance, with every lie. She felt so alone, no one was in the same situation. Fatua wished very much not to endure this kind of loneliness any longer, after all, she was always surrounded by all these fairies, but still so isolated.

She had had enough, couldn't take it anymore, the colors of her wings, her dress were fading rapidly, and even her magical powers were waning. She wondered if she was cursed. She would have liked to get rid of those silly wings, that silly purple color. Tears streamed down her cheeks. She actually loved these colors. She stroked her skirt and was kind to herself again. When the tears had dried, she decided to leave the forest. She flew far away, further and further, until she was sure that she couldn't find her way back. She decided to land, and that's when she started to regret everything.

Suddenly, she heard a whisper, 'Fatua?' She was startled by the faintest of sounds and immediately took flight. But when she looked down, she couldn't believe her eyes. A fairy waved at her. The fairy seemed to full of joy. A fairy who looked almost exactly like her, with purple wings and a lavender dress. 'Fatua, you don't have to be afraid.' She flew towards her. 'I'm Fahmiya. We were wondering when you would finally find your way to us.' Fatua told her story, listened to Fahmiya's, and couldn't stop talking. Only much later did she realize that she didn't have to lie, she realized that Fahmiya believed her.

"They exist, but they don't want to show you their true face because you don't deserve it."
Alfred Kinsey

Do you really think she knows?

Sometimes, you can see it in the most inconspicuous gestures, the invisible nuances of differences, and at some point, a single glance is enough. When this happens, one is lucky or has unwittingly stepped into a, perhaps perpetually enduring, time loop. The same looks, words, and fleeting touches don't lead one out but only deeper in. Everything is so obvious, yet one can't break free. Wishing her a beautiful day, while you want to cry. As much as you desire her to experience this lovely day, you are unable to bestow it upon her. Despite the willingness to do anything, you remain confined to only trying to speak this wish into existence. Actions are not appropriate. Observation is possible only from behind the blinds, not for long, as one doesn't want to admit to the role of a clandestine observer. Every other role is taken or promised to someone else. None of the roles would fit; they would need to be rewritten.

Two pairs of eyes, hard to distinguish, nearly melded. Even in separation, parts of them will forever stick on each other. These gazes will never fully detach; they will endure. They are destined to.

I had chosen her, I simply couldn't see the way out anymore. I didn't feel trapped; I finally felt safe.

„Sometimes there is no choice, you gotta be
the poet."

I'm wearing my red, although somewhat faded
sweatshirt. She's wearing that green jacket
she sometimes lends me when I get too cold.
We're lying on the swing at the children's
playground next to our apartment building.
It's one of the first summer days, but we both
know that I won't be around for much longer,
that we won't be roommates anymore. 'Two
weeks,' she sighs. I just nod, turn to her, and
look at her. 'What happens to all our plans
now? In my head, we've experienced so much
more. I remember some things as if they
really happened; I've thought about them so
often.' Not only often, but also in great detail.
'If we could tick off one item from our list,
what would it be?' she asks me. 'Hmm.'
Actually, I don't need to think about it.
'Probably, driving to the beach and listen to
the waves together.' It sounds clichéd, and yet
I can't imagine anything more special. 'Then
let's do it today.' She smiles. She's not just
smiling with her mouth but also with her
eyes. 'Really?' I'm hesitant, not wanting to
allow myself to be happy because I wouldn't
be able to handle the disappointment. 'Really.
I'll just call in sick tomorrow.' She smiles even
wider because she knows I wouldn't have
expected that. She usually follows all the

18

rules. 'Well, you've been going to work sick so often, you can stay healthy at home now.' She jumps up first, then reaches out her hand to me. We quickly pack everything we might need into shopping bags and then into the trunk. It's 8pm, and we head to the nearest supermarket, going overboard and grabbing anything that even remotely appeals to us. The shopping ends up on the backseat because the trunk is already full. She takes only the two bottles of iced tea with her to the front. We drive for just an hour and fifteen minutes, not nearly long enough to listen to all the songs that come to mind during these car rides. We stop at the first piece of beach we see. Of course, the sun is just setting, it can't be real, but everything is golden. It looks a bit as if the sea is on fire. We take a quick dip in the water, lay our wet clothes on the car roof, pretending we're not in France but in Southern Italy.

Then we lay out everything we got from the supermarket on the blanket, and she pulls out a battery-operated string of lights from one of the many bags. I look at her as if she's just fulfilled my greatest wish (which she probably has). I want to take a picture of everything, want her to be in it too, but she hates having her picture taken. We fall asleep on our yoga mats and in our sleeping bags. Then I wake up, not knowing where I am, wanting to turn to her, be closer to her. I turn around, and there's no one there. I'm in my new apartment, in my old bed. It was just longing again, another unjustly placed memory of the unexperienced. I'm wide awake, not too sleepy to believe I'm really at the beach. If only I hadn't turned around, if I could have resisted, then I might have gone back into the dream, back to her.

I spoke into the phone, asked for her, yet no
one knew her, no one knew this name. She
had told me that her name was Claire, that
her last name meant circling sea.

She had also told me her secrets, her deepest
thoughts.
I knew her biggest fears but not her name.

I took the bus, the train, or my car, and I was in love with her. I traveled around, and even the gray city outskirts felt like a magical place.

What you can tell her

I've known Ben since my childhood. Our parents were friends, we shared Italian vacations, the usual. Even though we're the same age, I can't believe he's in love now, truly in love, I guess.

'How should I tell her that I can't just be friends with her anymore?'

'Hint at it first, don't rush in with it,' I advise him. He's in love with Laura. She's not just likable, beautiful, or funny, there is something magical about her, as if she came from a fairy family.

'But what do you say exactly?' he asks.

'If I were you, I'd tell her that she makes you feel like your playlist, the one you created especially for those rare days between spring and summer. But what do I know?'

'I don't know if that fits, and besides, it would be a lie.'

'Well, then, I'd tell her that you want to read all the books she likes, just so you can see the world from a perspective she can identify with.'

Bens's look says it all.

It's not easy for me to give these tips to him, especially.

'But you're probably too shy to say that, aren't you? Probably find it difficult, am I right?'

'No, why would I? I just need a little guidance,' he says.

'You can tell her that you think of her when the sky is pink or orange. Or when you're eating really good cake. Or that you believe what's between you is as gentle as the sound of a hairpin landing on the ground.' I couldn't stop philosophizing.

'Oh Eloise, it doesn't surprise me that you don't have a boyfriend,' he jokes.

'Then tell her that you never thought you'd find yourself in a style that isn't your own, that you're addicted to learning more about it. Or that you wish you were the wind, so you could play with her hair too. That's all I can think of.'

That's not true. After all, I'm not Ben.

'Let it be. I'll figure it out somehow tomorrow. I'll just tell her at the party.'

'Well then, good luck.'

Eloise sat in the small anteroom of the club. She sat on the windowsill, staring at the wall. At some point, absentmindedly, she reached into her bag. She threw a hairpin on the floor. First one, then the second, then the whole pack. No one looked at her, no one wondered what she was doing. No one seemed to see her, and no one seemed to hear the hairpins. She picked them all up again, sniffling. Only to throw them all with full force against the window, and even that didn't interest any of them. They were inattentive, preoccupied with themselves. She went back inside. She stopped at the counter and watched as Ben kissed Laura. And as much as she wanted to look away, it had been impossible. 'He's not into you. There's no need to keep looking over there,' Laura's best friend shouted in her ear. Eloise just laughed. 'Why are you laughing so wickedly? You really think you have a chance with him, don't you?' She just wanted to get away. She turned around and rummaged in her bag. When she looked up again, Laura's friend threw a drink in her face. Much worse than the drink was the demeaning, almost disgusted look. She proudly watched as Eloise touched her wet hair. Laura understood what had happened, looked confused and so unsure. Ben, on the other hand, hadn't noticed anything. Eloise held onto her phone. Once again, the desire flared up in her to throw her phone against the glass display behind the bar. She longed to see the glass shatter. Suddenly, she jumped up, clutching her phone in her left hand. She couldn't help herself. She threw the phone with all her might against the display. Everything shattered beautifully, just as if all the glasses were breaking in relief. For the first time that evening, she had no tears in her eyes, and for a brief moment, everything was okay. She would do it again and again, she thought. The bartender continued mixing drinks, everyone danced, no one looked at her, not even Laura. Among the shards lay her intact phone. She reached for it and left wordlessly. She imagined how everyone would yell at her, how she could be the cause of annoyance, of some other's emotion. On so many days, she wished for a loop of screams that you could play loudly through headphones. The small splinters made her hands look like a bloody starry sky, as if a delicate rose had been violently uprooted.

Outside, she looked at her hands again, they were unharmed. No one saw her anger, her suffering, her hope. Her rebellion was invisible, ineffective. No one noticed it. She felt like she couldn't do more, be louder, brighter, more exposed, yet all her efforts went unnoticed. She felt nothing, only the wet strands on her face. Tears ran hotly over her skin. It didn't look like she was crying; it looked like her eyes were simply overflowing.

I saw her and immediately felt overwhelmed, in the best way. I knew that nothing comparable had ever happened to me. And I also knew that something from that moment would echo within me forever.

Cut

I keep returning to our places over and over, searching for clues as to why you left, why I could leave. It's raining there. It smells like wet wood, and you're no longer there. I search for you in my memories, try to learn new things about you without ever seeing you, without ever speaking of you. I miss them much more than I can even imagine them anymore. Sometimes I meet them in a dream, then I find answers, have a rough sense of how they are doing. Otherwise, I consciously choose memories because they obey me, let me feel the way I want, and promise to be a kind of abandoned, inaccessible future. Every time you relive a memory, it changes, as if you're diluting a drink more and more. In the end, it has nothing to do with what it once was. And yet, I remember everything with unbearable accuracy.

Because you cut deep, nothing went deeper. Since you've been gone, I've been trying to heal the wound all by myself. When you don't seek help for particularly deep wounds, it's as reckless as trying to fix a broken bone on your own. Sooner or later, everything will heal, but most likely crookedly. Then you have trouble moving normally, you limp, you don't dare to run quickly, you no longer jump. You become cautious in the saddest way. Life loses its

28

excitement because it is consciously suppressed.

A breakup is like a death, with the difference that it exclusively concerns you. You fell in love with a version of a person that no longer exists, blame yourself for possibly being at fault. Not only does someone seem dead, but you also have in the back of your mind that others may still get to know this version, perhaps even persuade it to stay with them longer.

I made peace with the fact that you took all the paintings with you, learned to enjoy their frames, had to get used to it. I didn't really have much of a choice. Even though the pictures are gone, their frames hold the memories of all the colors, of all the imprecise, blurred brushstrokes.

Yet, I can't help but wonder what you would have done or rather said if you had really known me, if I had known myself better at that time. Maybe you wouldn't have believed me, maybe you would have found yourself in my secrets. Perhaps there would have been no room for further revelations in the rubble. On the other hand, we might have found roots of chaos.

Because what you said never made patterns.

Everything seemed so exciting, so colorful.

Without patterns, you never know how something continues, how something goes on.

Eventually, the colors fade, the excitement no longer carries you, at some point, it just doesn't continue.

And if this love was everything, then I will spend the rest of my life reliving it over and over, the way I wanted it to be, the way it wasn't allowed to be. Because I didn't suddenly disappear, you could watch the rain gradually dissolve me. And even though it was torturous, so terribly cold, and progress was painfully slow, it was right.

In short, leaving was cruel, but loving them was crueler.

Two pairs of eyes, hard to distinguish, nearly melded. Even in separation, parts of them will forever stick on each other. These gazes will never fully detach; they will endure. They are destined to.

This time, everything was different because I liked her and didn't just want to please her. I didn't just want her to like me; I wanted to like her too. Everything was different because I didn't have to send hundreds of explanations ahead. She understood me, and I understood her. For the first time, a person I was in love with spoke the same language as me. No one felt like too much or had to hold back; everything was fine, everything was so wonderful.

I wrote you a love letter and hid it.

I'd rather remain silent for the rest of my life,
I'd rather admire her from a distance forever
than scare her away with an impulsive action.

Orange

It was the first day of our visit when we began to feel somewhat settled. On this day, we had let the calm settle in. Most tasks were completed, we only needed to go to the store to buy supplies for the Seder evening. Robert's host family was celebrating the Passover, and we were to be part of it. Most people here had no knowledge of Jewish holidays, but there was something peaceful in the air, the contentment of an upcoming celebration.

"What else do we need?" Davina asked. "Paper napkins and an orange. The napkins aren't all that important, but the orange is," I explained. I wandered through the fruit section, and my eyes unexpectedly locked onto a familiar face. As I approached, I waved to signal my recognition, but she didn't seem to acknowledge me. "Hey, we know each other, don't we?" The woman looked at me suspiciously. "You're a friend of Dorothy, right?"

"No?" The skepticism in her voice reverberated in my ears. "I most definitely do not know anyone named Dorothy." "Okay, then I must have confused you. I'm sorry." As I continued, I saw her turning to whisper something to someone while keeping her eyes on me. I got nervous, not understanding why suddenly everyone was talking in hushed voices, with their eyes on me.

And then, everything happened so quickly. They came for me, walking up to me, ready to do whatever was necessary, their faces expressionless as if they were remote-controlled. My heart raced faster than I ever thought possible. Everything was silent, everything was loud, none of it felt real. It happened so abruptly, so cruelly routine. No one explained to me what had happened, what I had done wrong. Robert and Davina screamed, pleading with the people in the supermarket for help, but none of them looked up. Then they were held back themselves. I don't know where they were taken.

And since then, I sit here, trying to remember how many days have passed, wondering what will happen, questioning what I did wrong and why it was wrong. I am underground, but there's a small window at ground level. In the spring, a little violet bloomed there. At its sight, I keep thinking about how many people may have experienced the same fate.

The kiss ruined me. It had the power to break me and build me up, all at the same time.

It's never easy, it's always about searching for signs, sending the right sings, it's about showing of what you are, and it's about strategically hiding it
It's about being so careful in your unmistakable directness
And sometimes not even the one who should be alike, get it, sometimes no one gets it, not even you

Walk in their shoes

She ran and ran. Continuously, further and further. She gasped and trembled. "What are you doing? No one is chasing you," they asked and said. But she continued to run, getting faster. Fear drove her, well aware that only she could feel the danger. Her heart pumped so circulating blood through her body, kindly and tirelessly. Her red shoes were long broken, yet she remained the girl in red.

"The girl has been running for years, and no one knows why," they whispered behind closed hands. She seemed to have gone crazy; she could have chosen a different life, a life where running wasn't necessary.

From time to time, she screamed loudly for help, her throat was sore, but no one seemed to notice, no one heard her, no one understood her. It was as if she were speaking a language that had never been taught anywhere.

She wished for, demanded, and longed for peace, yet she couldn't stop running. Perhaps not even for her own safety, but for those who couldn't just take off running. For all those who were already chained and knew they would never escape. She ran because she couldn't bear that fact, driven by rage but also by desperation.

Moreover, it was arrogant to think that she could have simply stopped, not knowing whether she was pursuing something or not. Certainty is always borrowed.

Eventually, the fear diminished, yet she continued to run.

The girl acted according to her nature and refused to be labeled as cursed because of it. Not being able to stop running may seem like a curse, but in reality, it is not. She knew it was a gift to be able to run tirelessly and that it was unfairly stigmatized as an inability to sit still. Refusing to be tamed was the only right thing she could do, not just for others but also for herself.

And only once did she stop. This one time, she made sure that there were others running.

Platonic Love

It's a normal morning. Just because something has become normal doesn't mean you don't appreciate it every day. Because you're always aware that it's not really normal. We get up, ask what we dreamt, have our coffee. Even if the espresso maker is empty, we don't leave the kitchen. So far, so everyday. But with Lena, it's not. Every morning feels like you already know you'll miss it in the memory. "Goodbye, looking forward to tonight," she says, kisses her fingertips, waves to me with them. I head to the café, take a walk, research, write, and look forward to tonight. In between, I keep thinking about how she'll walk in the door, how we'll giggle together. I'm curious about what she'll tell me, can hardly wait to show her the first draft of a short story. I only tell her about it, only to her would I read it. I change the water of the flowers I gave her. I do it every day, delight in the fact that she doesn't know, and that she doesn't have to thank me for it. I bring her a bottle of Diet Coke from the store because I can't leave a supermarket without a little something for her.

I don't just like her; I like myself when she's around. It may sound cheesy, but my soul finds peace with her. When it gets too quiet, I think about our conversations. She's the only person with whom I don't want to make an effort, and yet, I dare to do exactly that.

She comes home, we have pasta with salt and margarine, chat and laugh while she tidies her room. Then she pulls out a can of Diet Coke from her bag for me, and I rush to the fridge. We squeal and get excited, as if we've made the discovery of the century. We go to sleep and look forward to tomorrow.

Everything about her left me mystified. It was as if I had suddenly shrunk and was chasing a fairy among giant flowers and grass. You don't trust your eyes, yet you don't want to rest until you can trust them. But you'll never be able to trust them. It will never become less magical. I hoped so much that I would be allowed to connect to this magic forever, that I would never have to return to my old world. I hoped that both of us would want to hide from everyone else forever. I wished to follow her in her magic forever, maybe even keep pace with it.

The braveness of the heart can not be seen by eyes.

Searching and Finding and Running and Waiting

We don't live in the age of the Renaissance, the strict religious Middle Ages, or other such cruel times. Yet, just one inch outside of what we've long accepted, we no longer feel safe. We feel pursued, judged, unnatural. All that we once celebrated with pride suddenly seems wrong. All at once, we wear a dress, a dress that reaches down to the ankles and conceals everything that makes us in poetry that's hard to decipher.

We feel alone, even though we know that others are going through something similar, maybe even the same. Over and over, we view ourselves through the eyes of others, wondering what would happen if everyone could see as clearly as we do. Every tear feels like a betrayal of oneself, of everyone else. What's so magical and pure also seems like a curse, and yet, we'd rather live under this curse than without that magic. Because this magic overwhelms us, shows us why we think and feel and want to create something. It strengthens intuition, even though we manage to question ourselves repeatedly. We betray our intuition, but it remains kind, warm-hearted, benevolent. I wish to carry this benevolence into the world, to reflect it and have it reflected back. But where do you seek it? Where do you find it? And when should you better stand up and retreat? Sometimes, it is then the 17th century. You sit there in an ankle-length dress and try to discover what you only know from within, in the outside world. You sit in the meadow and desperately search for the right flowers, for flowers that truly make you feel what you're trying to put into words, to better manifest it in reality. Yet, you can't find these flowers anywhere. Because you're looking for a green carnation. None of them are green, none of them make you feel. Because where you are, it cannot possibly grow.

It's not easy to run in ankle-length dresses, and yet, you will manage. Because despite everything, it's worth being brave. It's so worth it. So be kind to yourself, listen to your intuition, and never forget that you're not walking alone.

Printed in Great Britain
by Amazon

35865652R00030